Short Stories In Verse

WAYNE BOYLE

authorHOUSE®

AuthorHouse™
1663 Liberty Drive, Suite 200
Bloomington, IN 47403
www.authorhouse.com
Phone: 1-800-839-8640

© 2008 Wayne Boyle. All rights reserved. 2008

No part of this book may be reproduced, stored in a retrieval system, or transmitted by any means without the written permission of the author.

First published by AuthorHouse 9/10/2008

ISBN: 978-1-4343-6633-7 (sc)

Library of Congress Control Number: 2008901191
Printed in the United States of America
Bloomington, Indiana

This book is printed on acid-free paper.

Preface and Acknowledgments

If I can awaken a feeling, a sense or a warm moment in your life, this will be my reward.

Dedicated to the memory of Brian and Chris who like many others left this earth far too soon.

I would like to thank Ines Rogers for her patience in drawing the accompanying illustrations.

Contents

Preface and Acknowledgments v
The Freedom Of Poetry 1
The Sleeping Lover 3
The Little Red Wagon 5
The Loss I Mourn 7
The Obnoxious Man 9
The Woman I Never Knew 11
The Wedding Chapel & The Philosophical Old Man 13
The Wind 15
The Wife That Never Was 17
The Value Of A Friend 19
Women 21
Winter Memories 23
Thinking Of You 25
The Tree 27
The Woman I Thought Was In The Past 29
The Ships 31
The Search 33
The Sunset 35
The Street I Walk 37
The Soldier's Wife 39
The Story Of Yesterday 41
The Sandy Beach 43
The Reckoning 45
The Sailors 47
The Reading 49
The Passion 51
The Office Party 53
The Mirror 55
The Listener 57
Blue Eyes 59

Christmas 2001	61
The Kiss	63
The Hospital-Power Of A Smile	65
The Grass	67
The Hug	69
The Frightened Little Boy	71
The Dreamer	73
The Door	75
The Christmas Dinner	77
The Childhood	79
The Bar	81
The Art Of Giving	83
The Passing	85
Number 46	87
Listening To The Waves	89
The Funeral	91
Bluenose 11	93
A Walk Through Life	95
A Tear	97
42nd & 8th New York	99

"THE FREEDOM OF POETRY"

The Freedom Of Poetry

I can sit and write my thoughts
About anything I like
A truth that may or may not be
For no one will know but me

For within my poetry I can hide
A passion, a love, a caring that can be denied
For this is one of my deepest fears
Allowing others to see my internal tears

For my poems are very brief
Referencing a point in time
That may or may not be
But what I believe to be

For I am a true romantic you see
Believing that love is meant to be
A passion to be shared with thee
But who will really believe me

The Sleeping Lover

I sat there beside you
Watching you sleep
Listening to you breathe
Ever so deep

If I was to kiss your neck
Would you awaken unafraid
Comforted to know that I was there
As I gently stroke your hair

Or, should I just watch you sleep
Admiring the person I adore
While you gently explore
The depth and tranquility of sleep

You look very beautiful lying there
In a peaceful world without a care
So I will leave you there
Careful not to disturb a hair

For I will wait for you to awaken
So I can tell you how much I care
About a person who is very rare
And a love that remains unspoken

The Little Red Wagon

I always wanted one you see
But there was little probability
As poverty prevented me
From grasping the handle that always eluded me

Christmas after Christmas did pass
The little red wagon never appeared
And my internal tears never disappeared
As the little red wagon eluded my cheers

Although the wagon became symbolic
Of a childhood fraught with fears
Of a childhood empty of cheer
The little red wagon never did appear

As the childhood years did pass
Adulthood brought some cash
The toys appeared with a vengeance
Thank goodness the little red wagon never appeared

"The Loss I Mourn"

The Loss I Mourn

*It is not the loss of you I mourn
But the feelings for which you had reborn
I had seen the signs along the way
That we would not be together today*

*I chose to ignore my inner self
Seeing only what I thought could have been
Not believing what my eyes had seen
Always wishing for what might have been*

*For it is within this loss I can see
The journey that is ahead of me
Where I must look more carefully
As I try to find a partner for me*

*For my heart is heavy with pain
As I try to regain
A sense of balance in my life
As I continue to strive for a better life*

*For we will never meet again
And no one is to blame
For it is just a game you see
Trying to find the right partner for me*

The Obnoxious Man

I sat there in a bar
Watching the people from afar
Within time before me sat
A pair of retired old men having a chat

I listened intently as the conversation carried on
The man on the left ran on and on
The man on the right barely hung on
As the conversation was being held by one

His statements did reflect
An older man lost in time
His ponytail outstretched to touch the past
His tattered leather briefcase open yearning for the past

His character was pathetically portrayed
By a man who could not accept
The inevitable consequence of life
That no one can by-pass

To age gracefully is an art
To accept your life without regret
Is a feat left to the more fortunate
Like the man on the right, who gracefully said goodnight

The Woman I Never Knew

I sat in the barber's chair
And noticed a lady beside me
Her blue eyes did sparkle
Oh a beauty so rare

For glances were exchanged
And then so were words
But my thoughts I could not exchange
For after all, I did not even know her name

For she was very young you see
Reminding me of a time that used to be
For she had a beautiful personality
Oh what a shame too young for me

I walked away after we said goodbye
To the counter I went and had to turn my eye
There was a smile oh so warm
A gentleness that I did so adore

The Wedding Chapel & The Philosophical Old Man

If I should live to be 108
Will I still continue to date
Or will I accept my fate
As I never did find my true sole mate

Some people say it's never too late
But by then it may be hard to find a date
As all of my friends will be called "the late"
And my choices will fade as if by fate

Throughout the decades I have watched
As perfect marriages were botched
As couples could no longer find their way
Through life together, so they called it a day

So why then do newlyweds proclaim
An everlasting love that no one can disclaim
As their marriage vows also do exclaim
Yet, when failing in life and love they have no shame

They end a marriage and say, "no one is to blame"
So the moral of this rhyme is simple
Before you decide to become a couple
Look at love, life and marriage as a lot of trouble

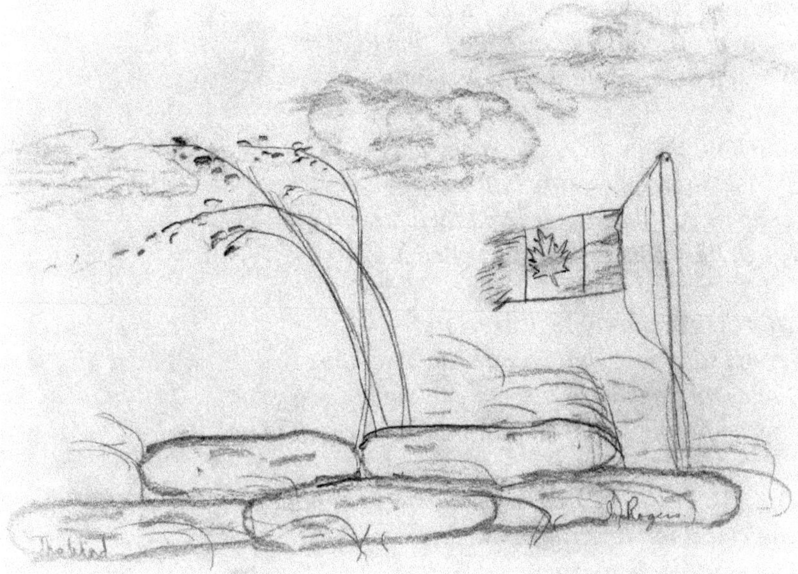

The Wind

*I listened to the wind
And envied its ability to travel
For where had it been
And where was it going*

*Could I accompany it along
For I am sure it would go
Where I had never been before
And where I would like to go*

*For life is like that you know
Never knowing where you will go
But always wanting to go
Where we end we will never know*

*For what will happen along the way
We do not know
Yet we continue to go
Life is like that you know*

*Just another breeze
In a life that will never cease
To look for another wind
Or perhaps another breeze*

The Wife That Never Was

I asked her to become my wife
Why, she said, this is a good life
For I never said yes
And I never said no

As a matter of fact
I just don't know
But I will let you know
I just don't know when

If I should continue to procrastinate
You will have to find another candidate
And then I'll have to date
Then again I will procrastinate

For I can't make up my mind
If you are the beau I had in mind
For there were others you see
Who had the same plan for me

If I sound confused
Don't be surprised
For it is in the mind you see
Not the heart you touch

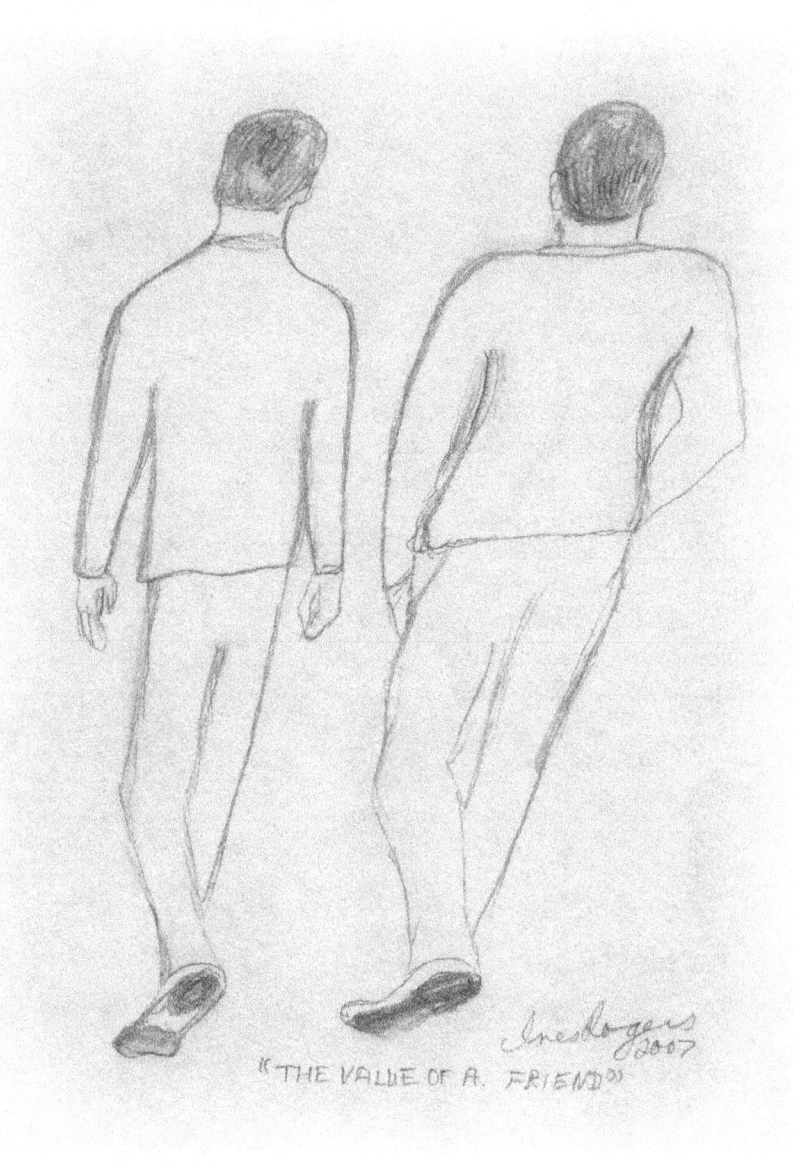

"THE VALUE OF A FRIEND"

The Value Of A Friend

For it is in friendship we find
A peace of mind
A value that cannot be expressed
In anything but warmth and tenderness

For a true friend is always there
Willing to show that they care
Never judging, just trying to be fair
Never forgetting, that they care

A true friend will never leave you alone
During a troubled time when no one is home
A cross word will never be spoken
As the trust is never broken

It is in this trust that we rely
On a friend not to deny
Us of our need to express
Our feelings, our wants, our tenderness

For it is in this friendship we rely
On a love that we can never deny
A word that never has to be spoken
As the trust is never broken

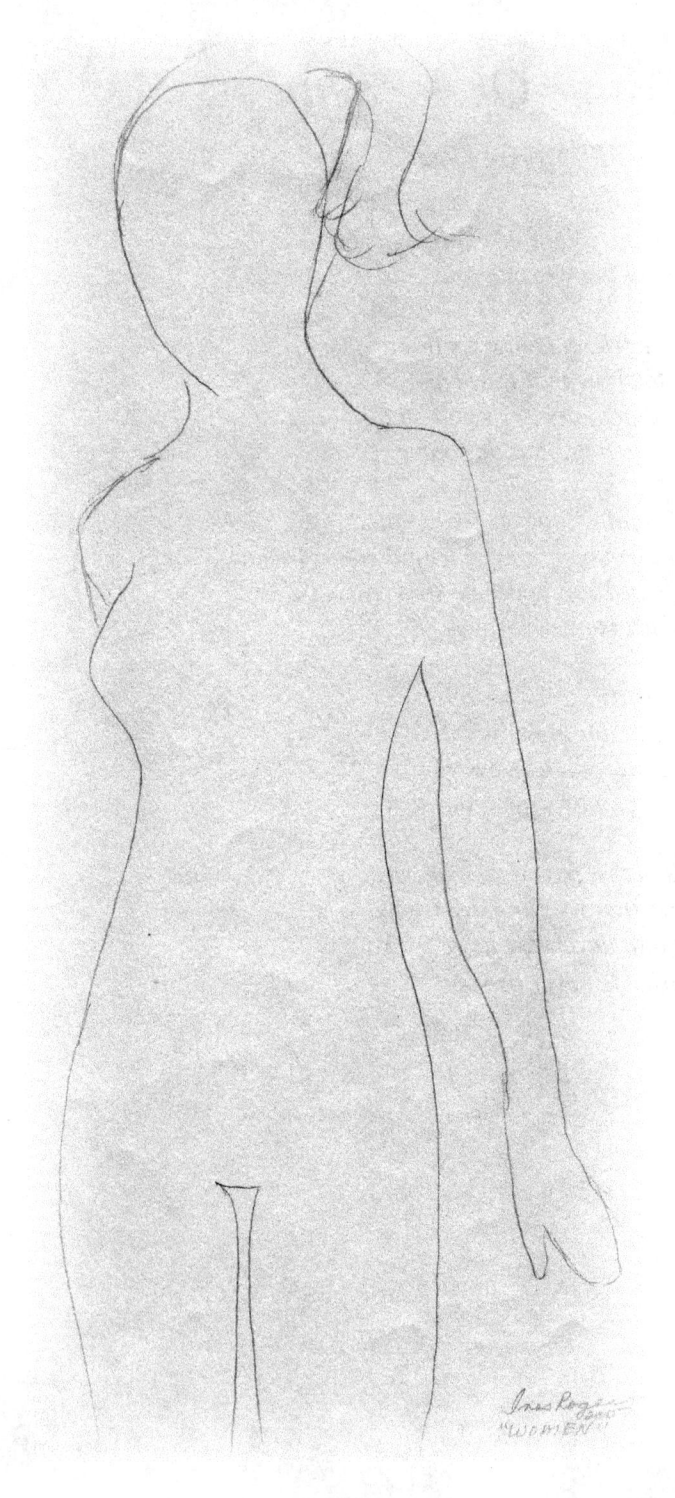

Women

It is within the pleasure of music
That my mind can find a place
To wander, to reflect, to contemplate
A life with little regret

I think about our times together
The warmth and tenderness of your touch
The beauty of your eyes that did reflect
A love, a caring, an innocent childishness

So humble, so empty, so much in love
With a woman who will never understand
The value of a love that is within hand
Until it is passed on to another hand

Like the laugh of a child
The cry of a loon, an eagle in flight
There is nothing that can replace
The words "I love you"

Winter Memories

I looked upon a frozen lake
As if by natures design
It was frozen in time
Capturing a moment in time

If only I could freeze my life
To a specific point in time
What a pleasure I would find
As again I would make you mine

As the ice reflects the cold
The setting sun provides no warmth
Except the memory of your touch
That I treasure so much

As the cold wind continues to blow across the deck
I hold my blanket to my neck
The warmth I feel can only be replaced
By the warmth and tenderness held within your face

It is with the greatest of pleasure
That I can grab this moment in time
As mother nature has provided me
The vehicle that reminded me of thee

Thinking Of You

When I am away from you
My mind projects an image of you
For this will have to do
As I am away from you

For the images I see
Are very pleasant for me
For they will have to do
Until I again see you

For it is in the anticipation
Where the greatest pleasure lies
As I anxiously await tonight
So I can hug you very tight

As the sun begins to set
I will whisper in your ear
Just simple sweet nothings
To alleviate all your fears

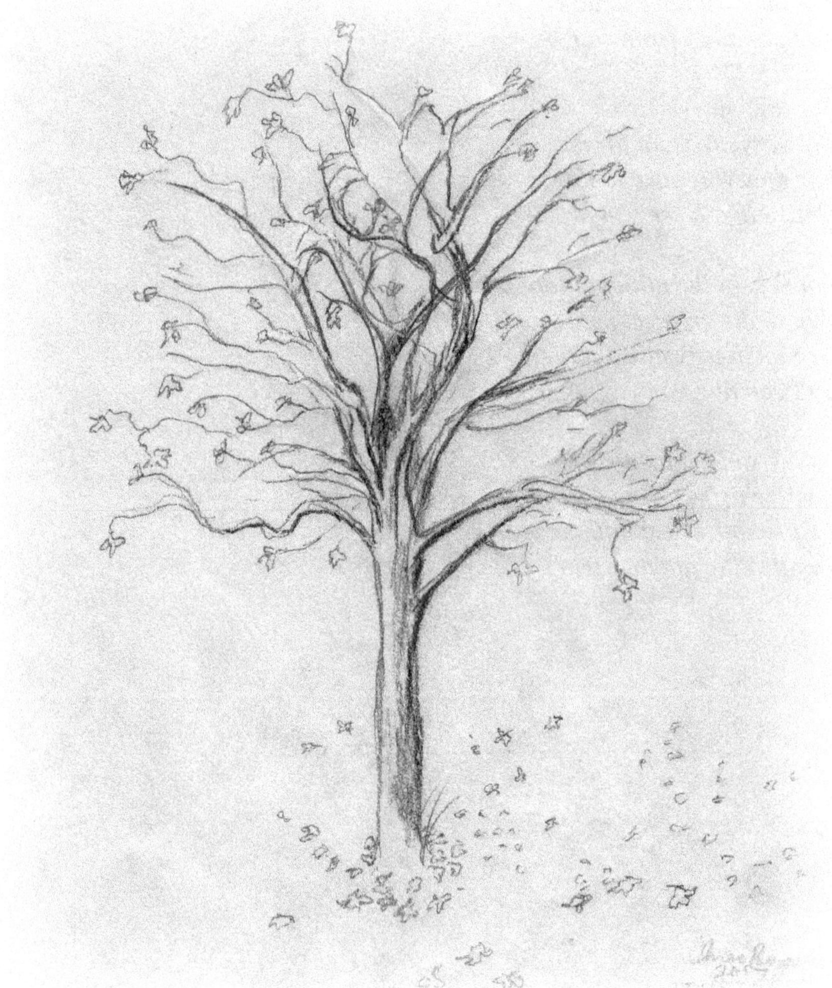

The Tree

The tree did bend upon the wind
Its leaves beckoning to the winds desire
To play, to frolic, to dance
To enjoy life at a glance

Never desiring anything
But to reflect a beauty
A colourful honesty
And a desire to be free

As the tree approaches the heavens
Its branches outstretched and leaves attached
She gracefully accepts
The sun the rain the stars and the moon

When fall approaches she provides
A colourful beauty that cannot be denied
As her leaves begin their decent
Another season comes to an end

For we will wait for the tree to awaken
So it can provide a beauty
That we all take for granted
Thank goodness she was planted

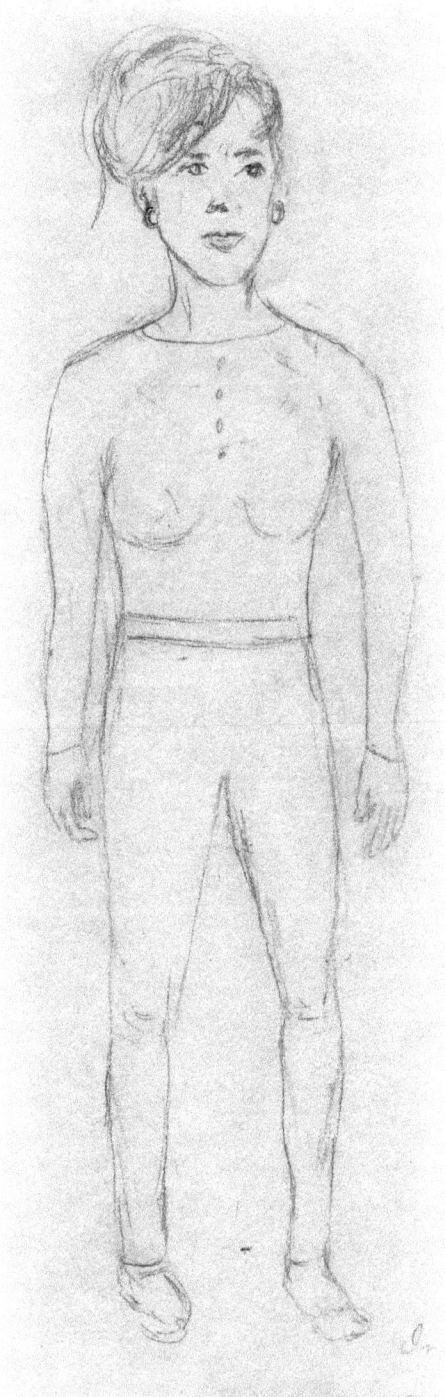

"THE WOMAN I THOUGHT"

The Woman I Thought Was In The Past

There was a woman that once I did love
Who had been out of my life for many years
Then suddenly did reappear
Jolting my memories, held so dear

For when we do review the past
We wonder why love did not last
Did we really try our best
Or are we just remembering the best

She looked very handsome standing there
Reminding me of a time when I really did care
When all I wanted was to hold her so dear
Remembering the past without any fears

While those days are definitely gone
I look back without any malice
Forward with only fond memories
Of a love now gone

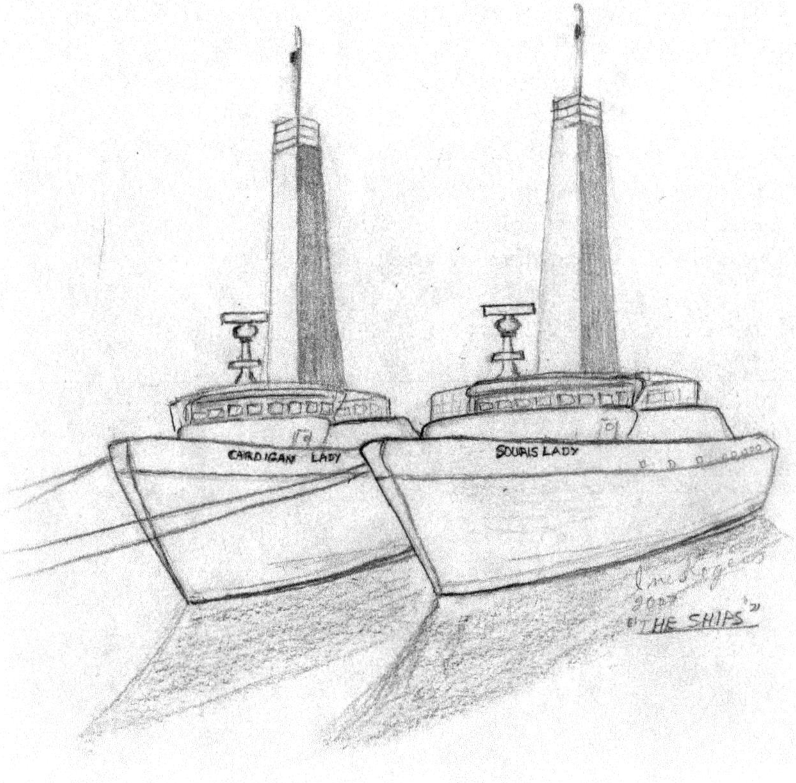
CARDIGAN LADY
SOURIS LADY
2007
"THE SHIPS"

The Ships

The two old fishing boats
Sat together proudly still afloat
Their huge black hulls did say
We've had better days

You could now only imagine
How proud they must have been
To slip in and out of port hardly seen
Their catch hidden within their hold

Yet, their current state does reflect
Hulls welded together by rust and time
Lines slack to accommodate the tide
Their purpose now undefined

Their wheelhouse standing proud
Their radar antennas waiting to turn
Their lights gleaming in the setting sun
Their spirit restless, wanting to move on

When the workaday world tells us were done
Will we sit idly by rusting away
Or, be thankful for today, appreciating yesterday
Looking forward to tomorrow, as if there was no yesterday

"THE SEARCH"

The Search

We spend our life searching
Sometimes with purpose
Sometimes without
But we never give up

For it is in the search
That we find peace
For that part of life
We could never find

For to stop searching
We would admit failure
With such an admission
We would never search again

For it is in this endless search
Be it for material wealth
A better life or just a friend
We decide the search must never end

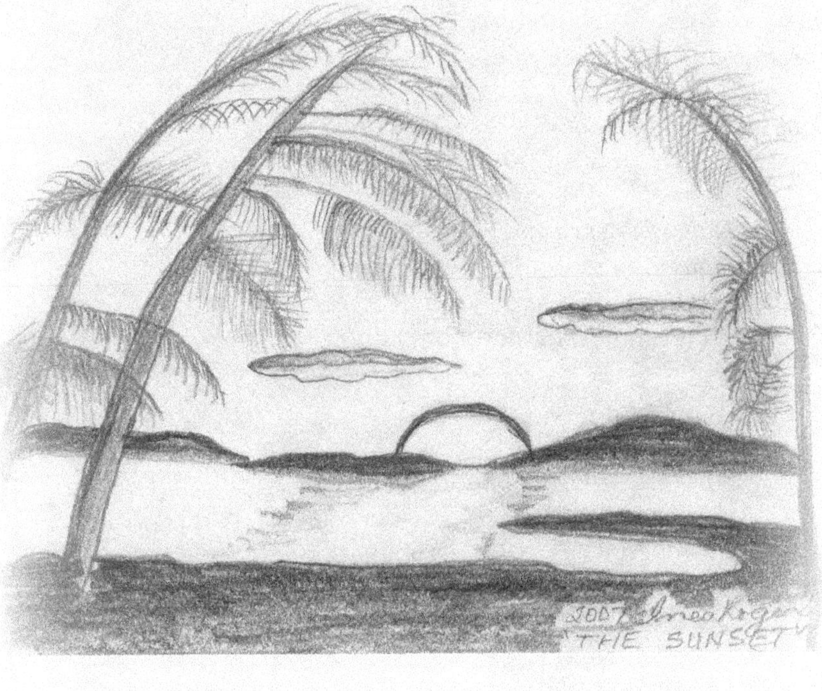
"THE SUNSET"

The Sunset

We sat and watched the sunset
Upon a lake we'll never forget
For this picture we cannot paint
Nor can a photograph reflect

The depth of beauty in the sky
Or the reflection seen by our eyes
And the warmth we feel inside
As we watch the sun subside

For as the sky does darken
The candle light inside
Provides the glow we require
To enjoy our time with the heart of our desire

The depth of beauty and warmth
Of the sunset we have witnessed
Can only be replaced by the
Warmth and beauty I feel within your caress

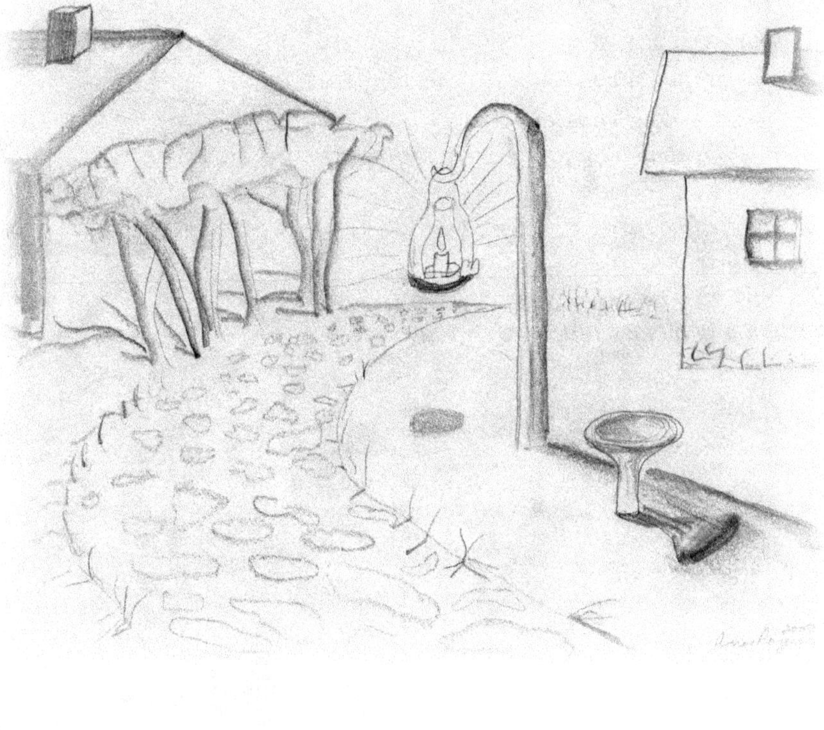

The Street I Walk

It is along this lonely street I walk
A single lamplight does flicker
To guide my way along
To where I do not know

The night sky is darkened
By clouds that are in abundance
By the absence of a star
Or a moon to guide me

For it is in the blackness I see
A life that lies ahead of me
For the cobblestones do paint
The path ahead of my feet

For no one said the street would be lit
Then why should I expect it,
For the guiding light is internal
To find it is eternal

For there are many streets unlit
We must walk as we progress
Through a life that is darkened
By others we try to impress

The Soldier's Wife

She sat there all alone
Looking very forlorn
She knew her lover would never come home
As she continued to stare across the empty room

His vacant chair did reflect
A memory of a happier time
With affection she recalled his words
"You will always be mine"

It was not his fault you see
That he cannot be here today
For a bullet did get in his way
As he was writing home, just like yesterday

Through her tears of sadness
She did reflect upon a life
Of hope and tenderness
Of a love once so freely given, now gone

She pulls her weak and sobbing body from her chair
To greet the guests who are there to share in her despair
She cries out that she will always care
But will my country still remember you my dear

The Story Of Yesterday

I miss the romance
That youth once did bring
Especially in the early spring
When my mind would begin wondering

If that pretty woman over there
Wouldn't mind if I continued to stare
At a beautiful creature
That is very rare

Or could I wander over her way
And let her know how I feel today
Or could we just please play
Or would she reject me right away

Well that won't happen today
As the women are no longer there to play
Like they were yesterday
Unfortunately my heart has never aged a day

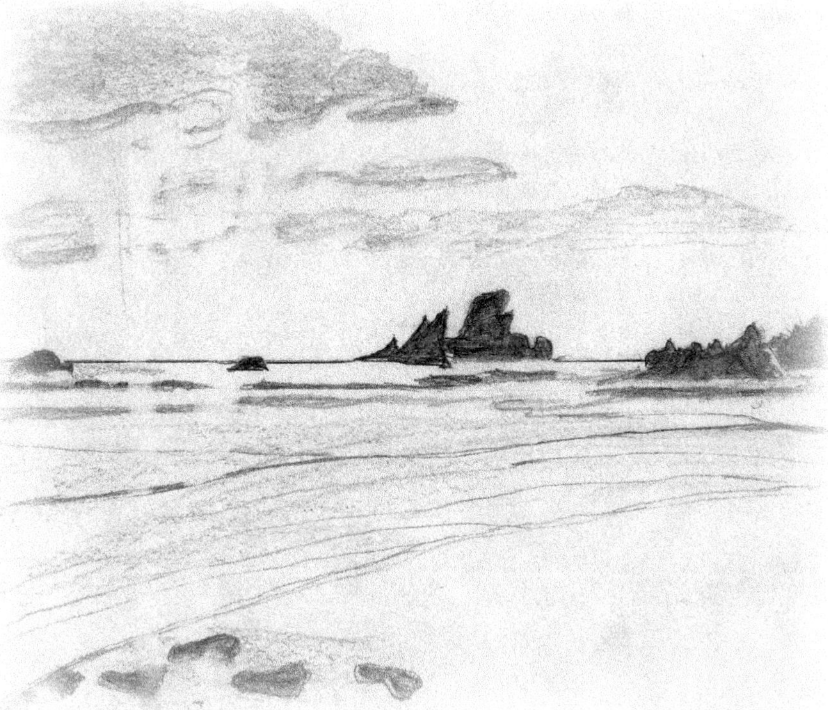

The Sandy Beach

When we walk along a sandy beach
And watch the waves beneath our feet
We see our footprints disappear
As the waves continue to reappear

As we walk through life
What impression do we leave
Do we just appear
Then quietly disappear

What can we leave behind
That others can use to find
A better way through life
With a lot less strife

What is beneath the sand we cannot see
What lies ahead we never know
But what we have today
We should never let go

The Reckoning

It is only a matter of time
That the woman I am with
Will want to become mine
At some point in time

What answer should I give
When she asks if I love her
For if I say I do not know
This answer she will take as a no

Can love be measured by time
Is it really something, we can control
Or does it just happen beyond our control
Or do we just wait for it to unfold

It is most unfortunate you see
That the answer to this riddle
Is far beyond me
While the reckoning is just ahead of me

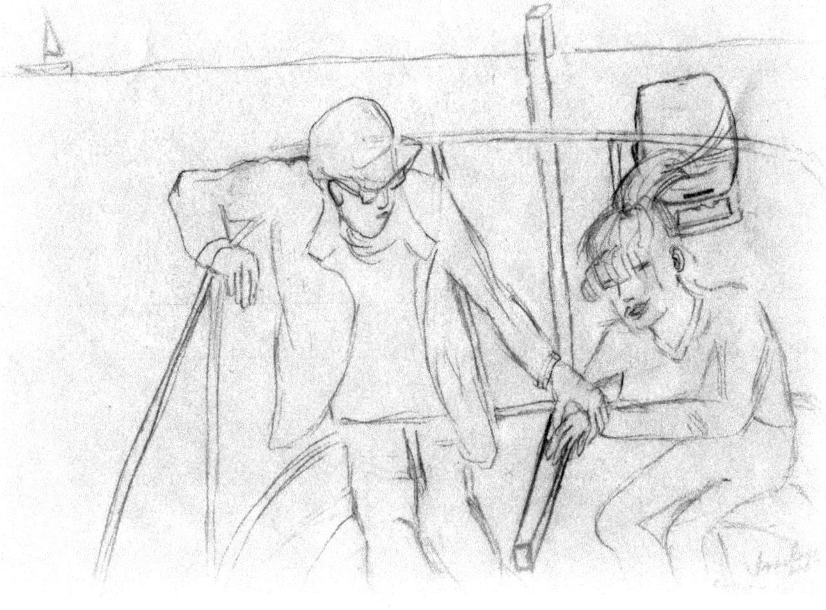

The Sailors

We set sail upon a lake
Where we had been many times before
Watching the wavers role towards the shore
Catching the wind, as we had done before

I looked at a face that beamed with delight
As we headed towards the wind so tight
I thanked my lucky stars
That she was here with me tonight

I looked into a pair of eyes
That reflected so beautifully the night
As we sailed along with great delight
Listening to the wind and waves in flight

I clutched her hand so tight
To let her know of my delight
That we were together tonight
And of a love that would never take flight

Within the depth of her expression
Was a love of sailing we shared
Nothing in life can be compared
To the two loves we both did share

The Reading

*How do I get into her mind
To understand her thoughts
When conversations are filtered
And my judgment is clouded*

*We look for signs as we listen
If the eyes are the windows to the sole
What do we really see
As mind readers we are not*

*It is in our judgments we must trust
For it is too soon to rely on trust
For we will continue to explore
Through conversation, the women we adore*

*For they are not meant to be read
Or meant to be understood
Just to be adored
And never ignored*

The Passion

I was once told to follow my passion
For within would be my destiny
Where I could fulfill my dreams
And find an inner peace

For this is very confusing
For you are never limited to one passion
So which one should I follow
For they are all valid

Therefore I tried them all
Some met with great success
Some with very little
But they are still mine

To live a life without passion
Would deprive yourself of inner peace
For there is no failure involved
Just the evolution of yourself

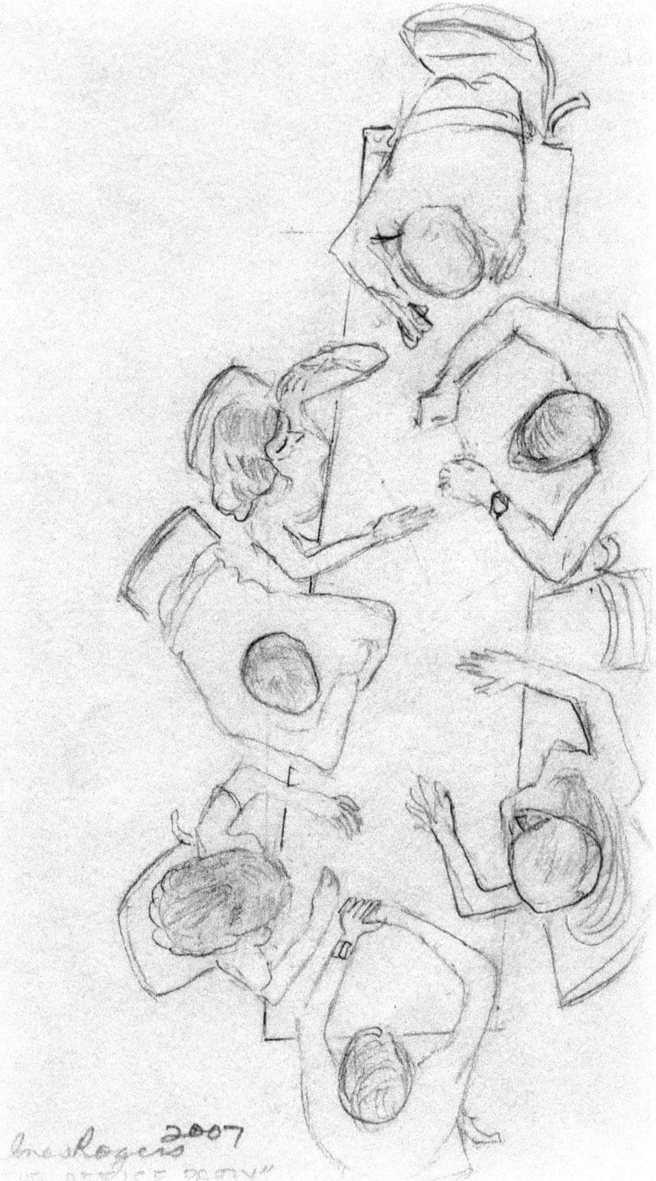
Ines Rogers 2007

The Office Party

I sat and watched as the guests did assemble
Their conversations although varied
Could be classified as office gabbing
Making no sense just general nonsense

There at one end was a handsome gentleman
In conversation with several women
His gestures did reflect a character
That presented no threat

The guests continued to assemble
Sitting with whom they felt comfortable
Sharing glances, managing smiles
As they sat and gazed around the table

Then arriving to sit in the last empty chair was an older gentleman
Encapsulated in a suit, looking stiff as if he did not fit
The character of the table and its guests
Evidenced by the silence that now did persist

So why do we attend
A party of very few true friends
Are we there just to say goodbye
Or do we really know why

The Mirror

When I look in the mirror
What do I see
Just a lot of over sensitivity
So I ask the mirror, what should I do

I could try to change
But that will not do
I could run away
To care another day

I am under a microscope you see
A more powerful mirror than you
She is looking for my faults you see
Instead of seeing the beauty within me

For perfect I will never be
So if you want to love me
Do it with all my faults
As they are a part of me

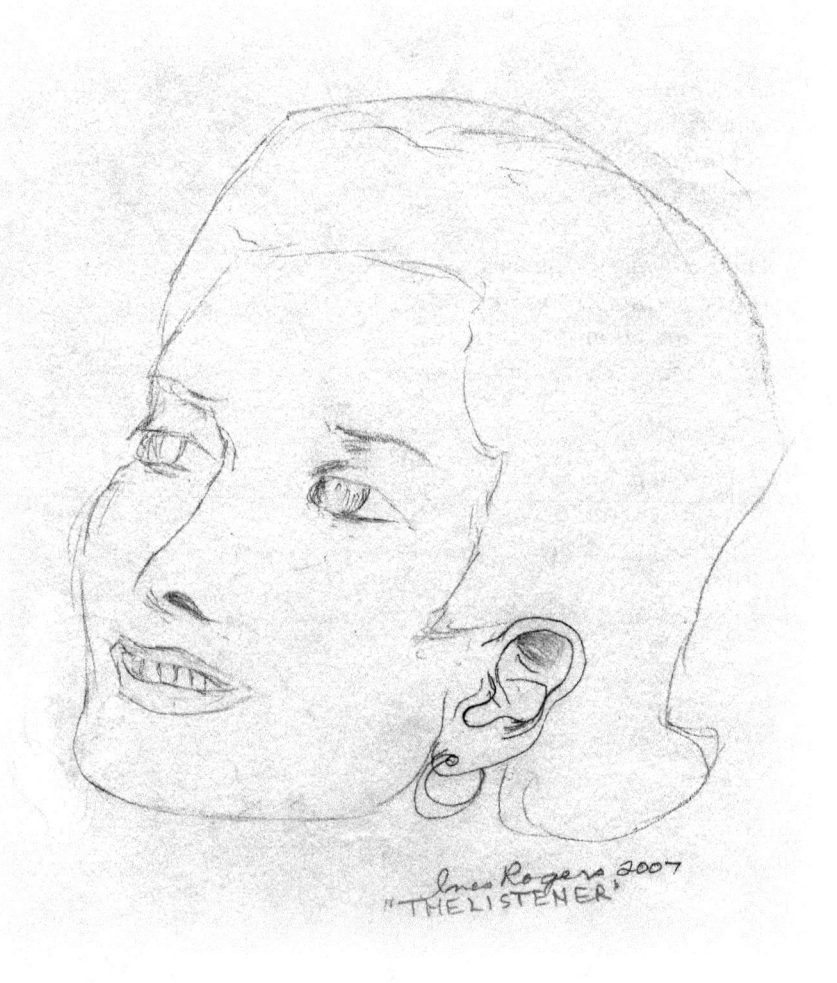

The Listener

*For an art that is all but gone
It was nice to find someone
Who could lend an ear
To a conversation so dear*

*For it is never in the content
That the listener becomes invaluable
But in their lack of comment
That help is wanted*

*For the listener must never judge
As that is not their purpose
Their purpose is to provide support
Not write a report*

*For listening is a two way street
What you give you get
What you hear you must forget
For repeating will be defeating*

"BLUE EYES"

Blue Eyes

I looked into a pair of blue eyes
That sparkled in the candlelight
To my greatest delight
What does this mean I wonder

Does she like what she sees
Do I meet her needs
Or is it just curriosity, I wonder
As the eyes continue to sparkle

If the eyes are the window to the sole
What does this sparkle reflect
Even my insecurity cannot detect
I like her you know, but will it grow

For the depth of beauty is in the eyes
Their strength is in the sole
Their character is in their passion
Yet love is in their heart

Christmas 2001

*For this is the first
That I have ever spent alone
Always taking for granted
That someone would be home*

*It is not the absence in the house
Of a love that once was present
But the realization of a fact
That love cannot be taken for granted*

*There is an emptiness that abounds
Even in a house so full
If its walls cannot echo
A love so ever present*

*For it is the simple things we ignore
In a life we try to explore
For it is in Christmas
That we expect so much*

The Kiss

I looked at a pair of lips
That I thought were in need of a kiss
I hesitated for a moment
Then they were gone

As I watched her walk away
I knew there would never be another day
For I hesitated you know
And lost the moment

For another pair of lips will come my way
I know not when
But when they do
I hope I will know what to do

For what is in a kiss
But warmth and tenderness
And a moment of heavenly bliss
Something we all miss

The Hospital-Power Of A Smile

I walked into the waiting room
And there I sat
In fear of the unknown
While feeling very alone

As I glanced up
A warm smile did greet me
From a beautiful young lady
Less than half my age

I thought she was very brave
To sit there all alone
Smiling so freely
So sweet, so tender, so pleasantly warm

When they called her name
She arose from her chair
The sweet warm smile did reappear
Washing away all my fears

The Grass

A man once told me
That the grass was greener
On the other side of the fence
Myth or truth I wondered

So I decided to venture out
I asked a nearby farmer
If I may wander about
Sure he said go ahead

So I began my trek
There standing before me
Was a strange obstacle
A ratty old fence

Then I began my climb
Step by step I clambered
Suddenly at the top
I fell, my God I thought

Am I alive or dead
It is then that I realized
That the grass is not greener
I am just wiser

The Hug

It is within the grasp of a hug
That we cannot deny
The fact that we rely
On the human contact that others supply

For it is in this hug we sense
An acceptance, an understanding
Of our needs and our recompense
For it is our desire not to be alone

For it is in the warmth of a hug that we believe
That we can find the security we need
Within the arms of someone we believe
To be a true friend indeed

For if within this hug is a true friend
Words may never need to be spoken
For the tightness of a hug is reassuring
And its sincerity never questioned

Although the hug may end
Its internal beauty will never end
As the warmth is never ending
And the conversations always beginning

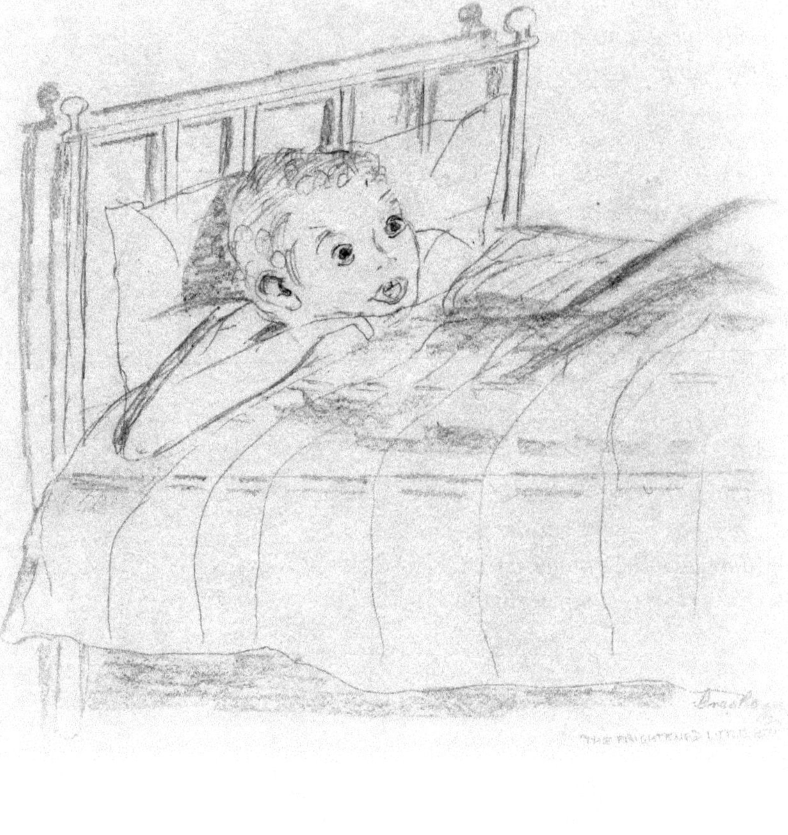
THE FRIGHTENED LITTLE

The Frightened Little Boy

I lie in my tiny bed
Knowing that another day is ahead
What will it bring I wonder
For a child this can be a frightening thing

For I am very secure in here
Afraid of what is out there
When I open the bedroom door
My secure little world will disappear

What will be there to greet me
A kind word, a hug, a kiss, perhaps
In an ideal world
But this is the real world

For the violence will begin
The insults will begin to fly
So I will take my tiny little body outside
To face a cruel world that is much kinder than inside

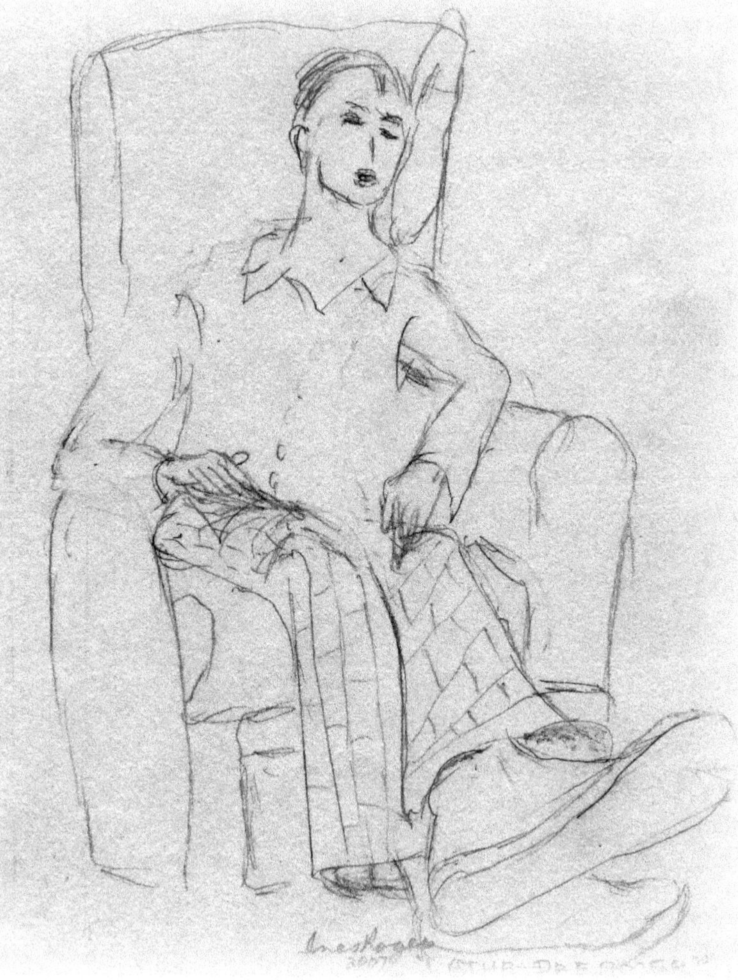

The Dreamer

*I lived a life
With little strife
As well, without a wife
For it was not that I did not try*

*For I failed you see and wonder why
Did I expect too much
Or not enough
Did I try too hard*

*Or did I just not know
Where to look
Or which one was right for me
So I will continue my fantasy*

*For there were many you see
Who have gone ahead without me
And I wonder how today they would be
If they would have stayed with me*

*For now I must continue along
As I am a dreamer you see
Therefore I will never be alone
For my memories will never leave*

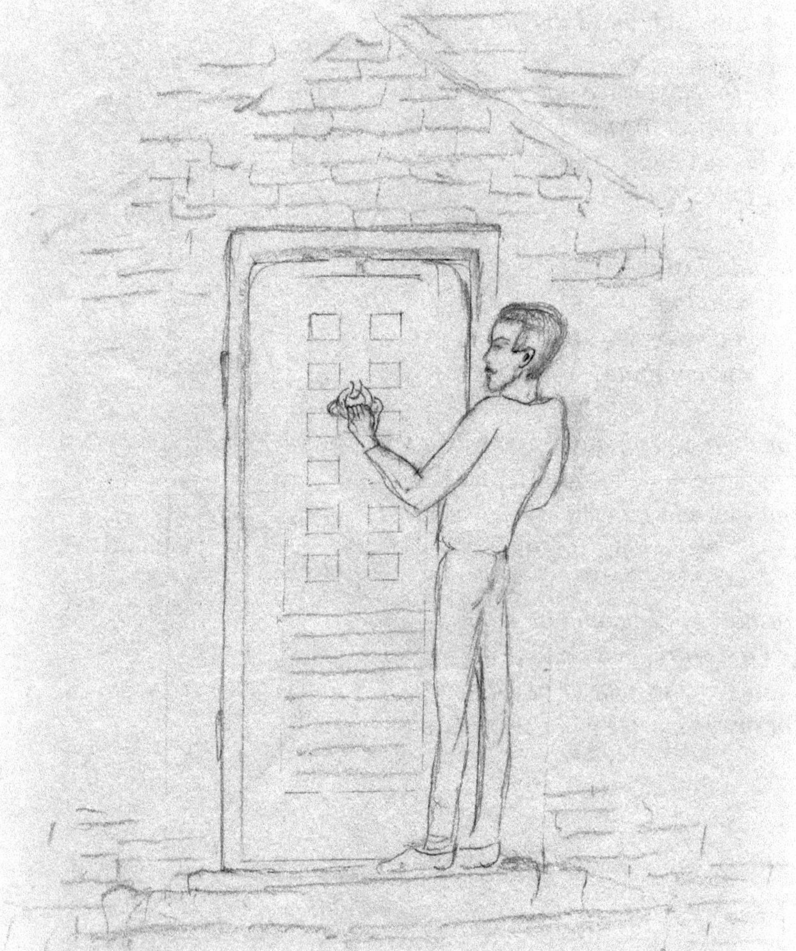

The Door

I knocked on a door
Where I've never been before
I did not know what to expect
A blonde or brunette

As the door became ajar
I gazed into a pair of eyes
That reflected a light
That would last all night

For I saw a face aglow
As pure as falling snow
A smile that would delight
And warm the night

To paint a picture so complete
Would not be an easy feat
For I saw a face I will never forget
But was she blonde or brunette

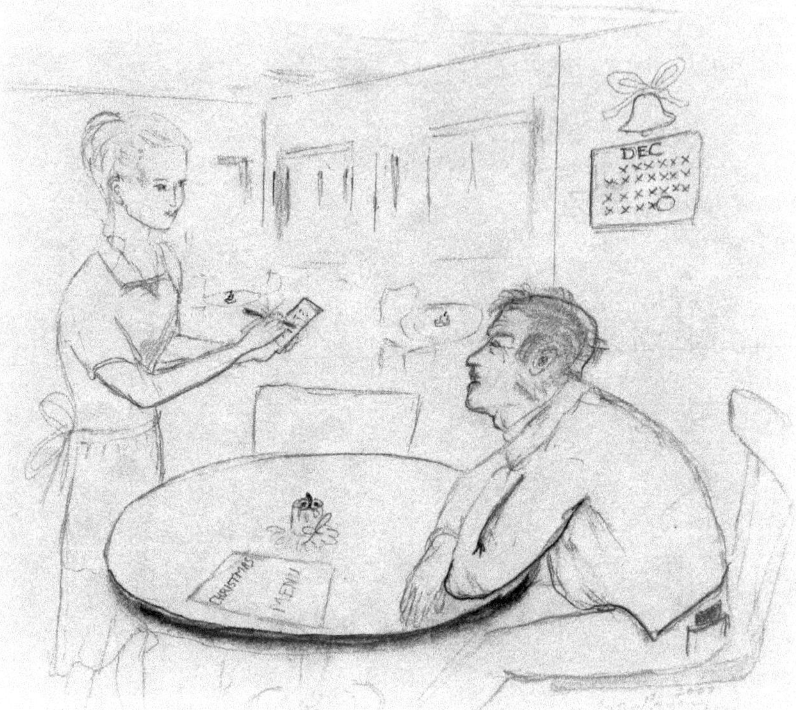
DEC
CHRISTMAS
MENU

The Christmas Dinner

The little old man sat quietly with his best tie on
The waitress asked "Dinner for one?"
He replied, most regrettably, "Yes my dear" as she quietly disappeared
For he knew she had no time to fill his lonely ear

He sat and gazed around the room
Listening to the noise of others pleasure
Remembering with great fondness
When he too was part of the noise

He reflected upon a prior time
When he and the love of his life shared some wine
Fondly remembering the glow of her smile
Which he knew would carry him, to his final mile

Just then upon his face appeared the greatest smile
Remembering all the times they shared
He quietly thought, I am not lonely my dear
Because all our years together time cannot erase

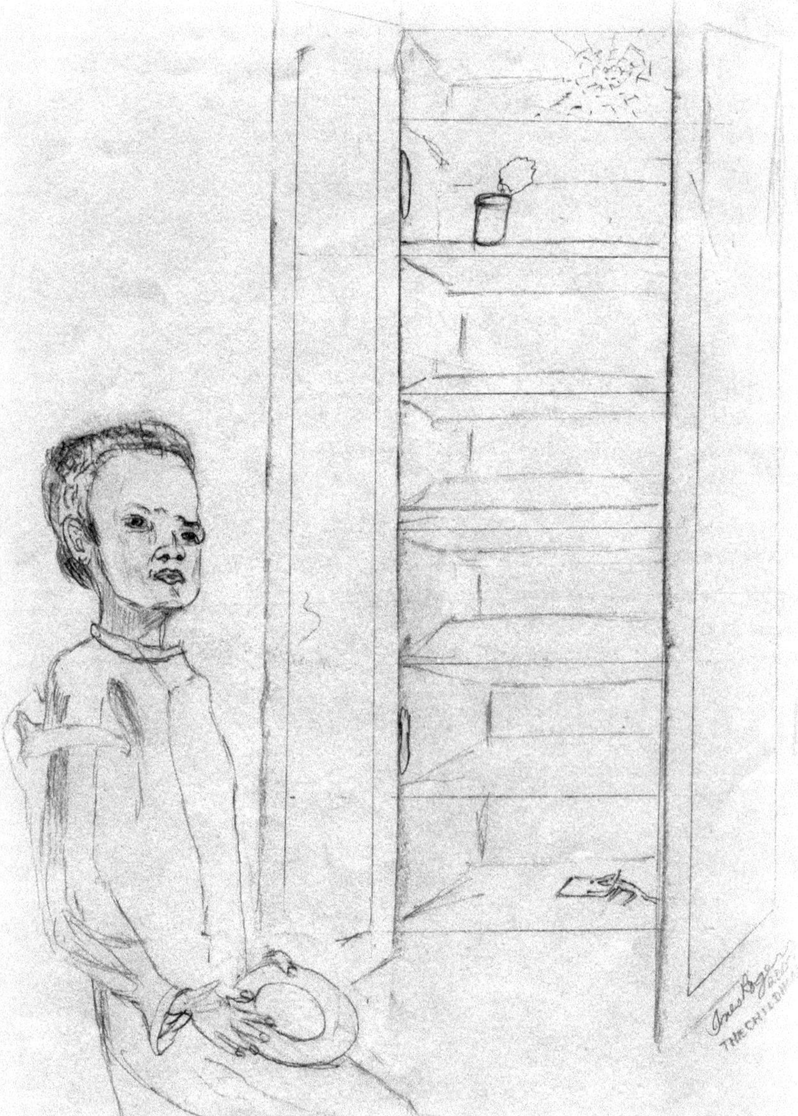

The Childhood

What would it be like to awaken
With the smell of mother baking
For the cupboard was bare you know
Even the mice could not grow

You lay about in the bed
Wondering what lie ahead
For this is a new day you know
What it will bring you never know

For we were never alone
We had our imaginations you know
But even they would not fill
A cupboard lying so still

We knew there were better days ahead
As long as we could awake unafraid
Of the future still unknown
And a life as pure as a child could know

If I could change the past
Would I last today
For it is in the past that today
I gain my strength for tomorrow

The Bar

I was to meet a woman
That was to arrive at seven
As I anxiously awaited her appearance
My eyes did wander

The woman beside me was far too young
My eyes did though see a fair form
Sitting in a corner all alone
Could that be her

Well I thought, again far too young
We exchanged glances
Then I thought, very nice
No, far too young

My eyes were anxiously watching the door
Disappointed that we were now past seven
Then I felt a touch, are you Wayne she asked
Now I am I said, as I saw an empty corner

The Art Of Giving

It is very difficult to give
In this complex world we live
As giving is an art
That comes from the heart

To give is to give of oneself
This task is difficult for many
But the rewards are a plenty
A practice that is not done by many

When you give from your heart
The rewards may not always be evident
Except in the heart of the recipient
But the smile you see will be rewarding

The warmth that you feel
Can never be duplicated
The responsibility never delegated
The need never lost

If I was to have a partner
That could give from their heart
I am sure we would never part
As two hearts are better than one

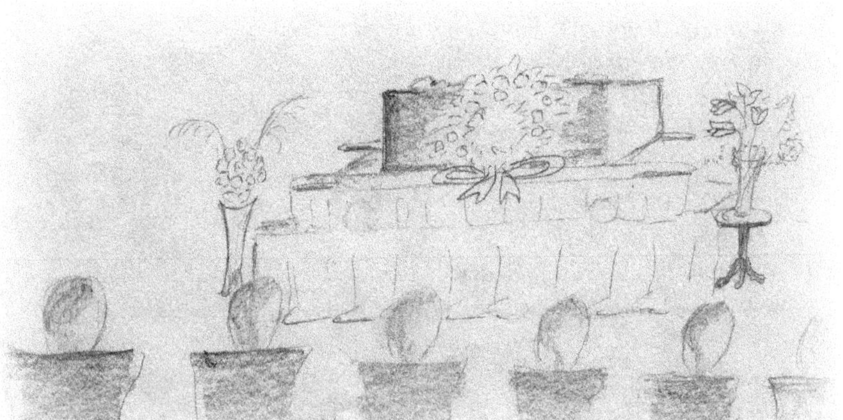

The Passing

I lay here before you
In my former state
Unfortunately, I cannot say goodbye
In my current state

Feel not for me
I beg of thee
For my life is gone
But my spirit lives on

Although my time here was short
Rest assured that I am in a better place
For heaven does not have the problems
Of your place

For we will meet again
In a world with far less pain
A sun that never sets
A life that never ends

There is no rent to pay
No dues to pay
Just a smile every day
And that's OK

Number 46

For I was to meet another woman
In another doughnut shop
For a coffee you see
And an easy exit may be

To my surprise there she sat
Such beautiful blue eyes
I will never forget
After all not an easy exit

To my greatest delight
I did not want to take flight
For the conversation I did adore
Perhaps the body even more

For in a world of disappointment
I met a woman that did not
For I could have talked all night
I certainly did not want to take flight

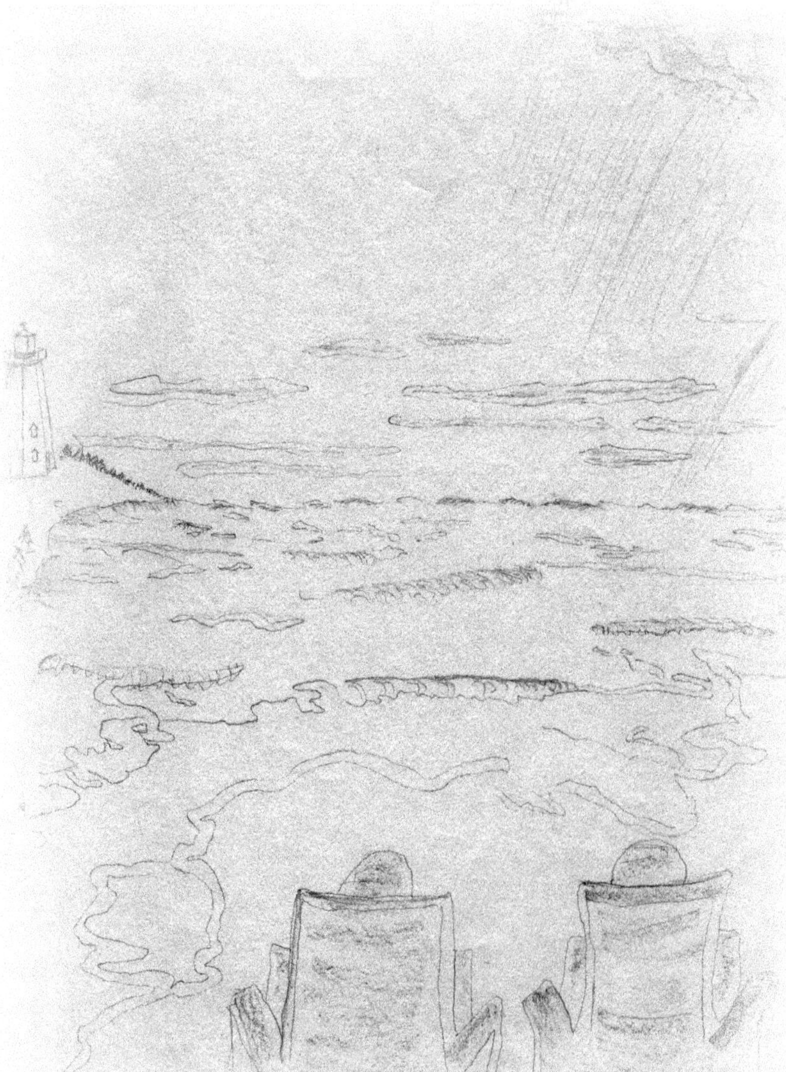

Listening To The Waves

I listen to the waves
Roll up upon the shore
For their journey has now ended
What stories could they tell

For they never remain silent
As know one asked them to
As they gently fall towards you
Then their beauty is upon you

For in the depth of a wave
Is a beauty that we can embrace
Whose life has ended we can accept
As a natural consequence

Of a life that has a purpose
To provide a beauty, a joy or just a toy
For us to play in and frolic in
As we cheerfully beckon them in

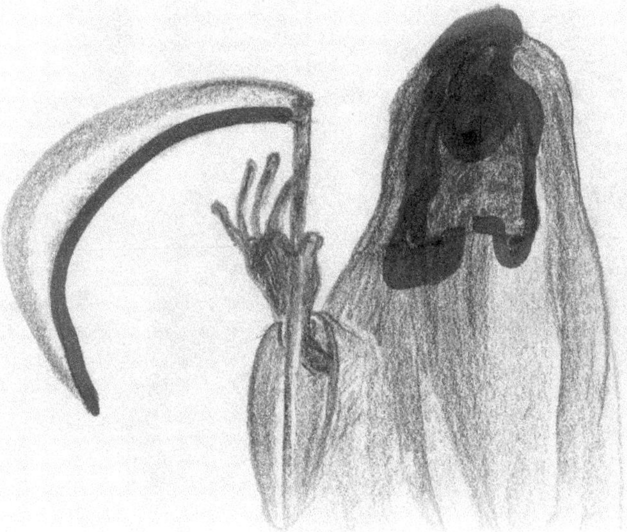

The Funeral

For it is in this mighty equalizer
That we seek a solace
As we become religious
And face our own mortality

If we pretend to elude
What a surprise we'll find
As death is never far behind
We are just one step ahead

Death is what we fear
Yet life is what we ignore
Taking for granted its core
Yet we are so close to deaths door

But we never really know
When death will wield its mighty blow
For our friends will all be gone
And we will be left all alone

Bluenose 11

I stood and gazed upon a sailing ship
Her topsides did reflect
A functional beauty
That only a true sailor could understand

If you let your mind wander
You could imagine her splendour
As she gracefully set sail
Upon an ocean swell

The decks did gleam in the daylight sun
Her fittings shone
With a pride few mortals achieve
Let alone ever see

Standing there before me
Was a crewman beaming with delight
As I admired her ship
She could have talked all night

The beauty of the ship
Was only surpassed by
The depth and beauty of
The youthful blue eyes my mind did caress

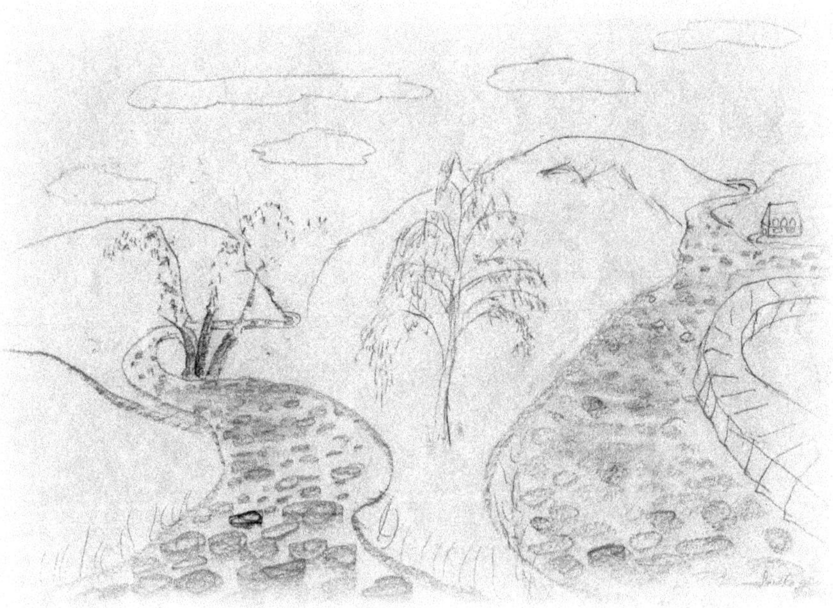

A Walk Through Life

I walked along a crooked road
Many paths did I take
Never knowing where I would end
But always anticipating a better end

For seldom did I find
The path I had in mind
Although none ended
They never were as I intended

If I continue my walk
What will I find
Another path, another place
Perhaps, but no more time

But what should I seek
For the path is never paved
With anything but my anticipations
And finally with my realizations

For another path awaits
As long as I have what it takes
To look, to seek, a better path
A better end
Perhaps a better life

A Tear

For what is in a tear
But a feeling, a release
Of emotions we hold so dear
Of the need for someone to share our fears

For a tear is something we hide
As a child we were told, it was undignified
To release the feelings we hide inside
In the form of a tear we continue to deny

For what we think is strength is a weakness
As we continue to fight
The release of a tear that we hold so tight
That will make all things right

For as a child we were taught
Or so we thought
Not to release our feelings in the form of tears
We held so taut

For a tear shed internally is a waste
As only you will see
The beauty held within thee
And your ability to be set free

42nd & 8th New York

I sat in a coffee shop
Observing a pair of newlyweds
As they stared upon a street
Filled with people they will never meet

I watched her warm glances head his way
As her face did display
The obvious love that was coming his way
For which she had no difficulty to display

He sat there with an arrogant look
That only youth and conceit could display
As he took for granted the love that came his way
Thinking that this is just another day

He never did return the glances sent his way
I wondered what he was thinking today
As the love may not be there another day
But, he was too young to know anyway

I watched them walk down the street
As their out stretched hands did meet
His head did bend to kiss her cheek
It was then I realized, all might not be so bleak

CPSIA information can be obtained
at www.ICGtesting.com
Printed in the USA
BVHW071749300621
610781BV00001B/100

9 781434 366337